A. Beasty Bites

B. Jungle Java

C. Savanna Library

D. House of Bones

E. Amazon Security

F. Everyday School

G. Wild'n Wooly Barber Shop

H. Arctic House Post Office

I. Monkey Bowl

J. Porpoise Pool

K. Big Cat Toys

L. Gator Grocery

Harley

Hayley

Pouch

Sarge

Midge

Pidge

Miss Bimble

To my grandson Travis, who adds joy to
my life and loves to read children's books.
—J. M.

ZONDERKIDZ

Every Which Way to Pray
Copyright © 2012 by Joyce Meyer
Illustrations © 2012 by Zondervan

Requests for information should be addressed to:

Zonderkidz, *Grand Rapids, Michigan 49530*

ISBN: 978-0-310-72317-2

Scriptures taken from the Holy Bible, *New International Reader's Version®, NIrV®.* Copyright© 1995, 1996, 1998 by Biblica, Inc.™ Used by permission of Zondervan. All rights reserved worldwide.

Any Internet addresses (websites, blogs, etc.) and telephone numbers printed in this book are offered as a resource. They are not intended in any way to be or imply an endorsement by Zondervan, nor does Zondervan vouch for the content of these sites and numbers for the life of this book.

Joyce Meyer is represented by Thomas J. Winters of Winters, King & Associates, Inc., Tulsa, Oklahoma.

Zonderkidz is a trademark of Zondervan.

Illustrator: Mary Sullivan
Contributors: Jill Gorey, Nancy Haller
Editor: Barbara Herndon
Art direction and design: Cindy Davis

Printed in China

11 12 13 14 /LPC/ 10 9 8 7 6 5 4 3 2 1

Every Which Way to Pray

Written by JOYCE MEYER
pictures by MARY SULLIVAN

Z ZONDER**kidz**

ZONDERVAN.com/
AUTHOR**TRACKER**
follow your favorite authors

It was a beautiful, sunshiny day, and the morning dew made Everyday Zoo sparkle. As Hayley and Harley Hippo scooted and skipped their way through the park, something in the distance caught Harley's eye.

"Look!" the little hippo shouted excitedly. "It's an angel!"

"I don't think that's an angel," said Hayley.
Harley moved closer for a better look.
"It's a duck!" he said with a pout.
Suddenly, a voice floated down from the rooftop.
"I'm a PELICAN!" the bird said. "Call me Pouch."

"I guess that's not heaven up there, is it?" said Harley, disappointed.

"No... but the view is heavenly," Pouch chuckled.

"At least you're closer to God up there," Hayley called out.

"We'll NEVER get that close to God," grumbled Harley. "Hippos can't fly or climb. We're stuck here on the ground."

"You don't have to be high in the sky to be close to God!" Pouch squawked.
"That's what prayer is for!"

Hayley and Harley looked surprised. They had always thought of prayer
as hard work. At least that's what it said in Harley's book.

"There are lots of rules for praying," Harley complained. "You have to do it just right."

"Says who?" asked Miss Bimble, who was on her way to the library.

As everyone gathered around Harley's book, the little hippo pointed to a page that showed a family, dressed in their best, praying in church. "Churches *are* wonderful places for praying," Miss Bimble said. "But they're not the *only* place to pray," Pouch added.

"And you certainly don't have to dress up every time you want to talk to God! At least I don't," Miss Bimble giggled sheepishly.

"Me neither!" Pouch grinned.

Pouch and Miss Bimble explained that you can pray anywhere.

On the train ...

at the library ...

underwater ...

even at the ice-cream shop!

"But, please!" cried Midge and Pidge, the town worrywarts who were out on their daily walk. "If you talk to God and eat ice cream at the same time— BE CAREFUL!"

"Good heavens, yes! You could bite your tongue!"

"Or accidentally stick some in your ear!"

"It could get very confusing, like patting your head and rubbing your stomach at the same time."

Harley turned to the next page in the book. "You read it," he said, handing the book to his sister. "It's got big words."

Hayley cleared her throat and read aloud: "Kneel down with bowed head and folded hands."

"Folded *hands*?!" declared Pidge.

"And you don't *have* to kneel, honey pie," said Midge.
"There are plenty of other ways to pray!" said Pidge.

"Bob and the gang like to pray...UPSIDE DOWN!" Pouch chimed in.

"What else does that book say?" asked Pidge.
"It says you should pray in a soft voice," Harley whispered.
"Otherwise known as your library voice," Miss Bimble nodded approvingly.

"Good for some, but not me," said Pouch, and he opened his beak as wide as he could and shouted...

"God doesn't care if your prayers are LOUD!!" Pouch boomed.
"Or soft!" Miss Bimble quickly interjected. "You don't even need to make a sound when you pray!"

Hayley continued reading, "When you pray, try to use special holy words."

Harley closed his eyes and began to pray, "Almighty God of thy most holy bounty of, uh, holiness ... Harold be thy name ..."

"The word is 'hallowed,' sweetie," Miss Bimble said, "but you don't need to pray using fancy words!"

Pouch told the hippos to talk to God like a friend.

"Talk to him like you would to each other," he suggested.

"We can't do that!" said Hayley. "Sometimes we talk about silly stuff!"

"That's okay," Pouch said. "God wants to hear from you, and I'm pretty sure he likes to laugh too!"

"But how do we know how long to talk to God?" Harley asked.

"Talk as long as you want," Pouch replied.

"You can pray all day and night...continually if you'd like," Miss Bimble explained.

"I can even pray with just one word," said Pouch.

Suddenly, Sarge, the local police chief, ran up to see what the commotion was all about.

"You in the red!" he barked at the crab. "Hit the road before I write you up!"

TWEET TWEET TWEET

Then, turning to the others, Sarge said, "So what's going on here?"

"We're talking about prayer, sir," said Harley. "We thought when you prayed it had to be perfect."

"Nonsense!" snapped Sarge. "Prayer is simple.
You talk. You listen. You praise. You thank. You ask advice.
You stay in touch with your Maker. Period. Get it?"

"Got it!"

"Oh, and one more thing," Sarge added. "It's got to come from here … your heart." Then he turned to the group. "Any questions?"

"No, that sums it up very nicely," Miss Bimble said.

Under Sarge's watchful eye the group said their good-byes,
leaving the two little hippos with their new friend Pouch.

"I'm glad we can pray any way we want," Harley said.
"Me too," agreed Hayley. "We can be LOUD ... or quiet!

We can kneel
or stand ...

or dance!

We can pray in the mud...

or in the tub!"

"But be VERY careful!" Midge called out across the park.
"Soap can be very slippery!!" added Pidge, as they continued on their way.

"So, what do we do with this?" asked Harley, holding up the book.

"I don't think you'll need that anymore," the pelican replied.

Hayley and Harley thanked Pouch for all his help, and then gave him a farewell hug.

As Pouch flew back to his perch, Harley
turned to his sister. "You were wrong," he said.
    "I know," Hayley replied with a smile.
"He really IS an angel!"